The Jam Street Puzzle

Margaret McAllister

Illustrated by
Tony Sumpter

OXFORD
UNIVERSITY PRESS

OXFORD

UNIVERSITY PRESS

Great Clarendon Street, Oxford OX2 6DP

Oxford University Press is a department of the University of Oxford.
It furthers the University's objective of excellence in research, scholarship,
and education by publishing worldwide in

Oxford New York

Auckland Bangkok Buenos Aires Cape Town Chennai
Dar es Salaam Delhi Hong Kong Istanbul Karachi Kolkata
Kuala Lumpur Madrid Melbourne Mexico City Mumbai Nairobi
São Paulo Shanghai Taipei Tokyo Toronto

with an associated company in Berlin

Oxford is a registered trade mark of Oxford University Press
in the UK and in certain other countries

British Library Cataloguing in Publication Data

Data available

ISBN 0 19 919496 3

3 5 7 9 10 8 6 4 2

Guided Reading Pack (6 of the same title): ISBN 0 19 919575 7
Mixed Pack (1 of 6 different titles): ISBN 0 19 919499 8
Class Pack (6 copies of 6 titles): ISBN 0 19 919500 5

Printed in Hong Kong

Contents

Chapter 1

"What's Happening?"

Aidan Vickers was nine years old and very popular. Everyone wanted to be his friend.

He wasn't rich, or very clever. He was all right at sports, but nothing special. He was a good friend, and he was nice to smaller kids. But what everybody really liked about Aidan was his mum's job.

Mrs Vickers ran the snack bar at
Jam Street football ground. Jam Street
was the home ground of Lowgate United
Football Club.

Everyone at Aidan's school supported
Lowgate. Sometimes Aidan got free
match tickets, so everybody liked him.

This season, strange things were
happening at Lowgate United.
Something at Jam Street was seriously
wrong.

Lowgate were having a great season. They never lost a home game. The goals they scored at Jam Street were impossible. That was the trouble: impossible.

If the goalie kicks the ball clear of the goal and it turns round and comes back, it's impossible. If it hits the post and still goes in, that's impossible.

If it's heading for the Lowgate goal, and then it stops in mid-air, falls down and rolls away, that's more than impossible. It's weird.

It looked as if Lowgate were cheating. But nobody could tell how it was done.

The away fans booed when the Lowgate players ran on to the pitch. And when the ball changed direction, they shouted, "Cheat! Cheat!"

Everyone was asking how Lowgate did it. Everyone wanted to know what was going on.

Lowgate's manager, Big Brian the Boss, crossed his heart and said on his word of honour that they weren't cheating. He said it to the fans, and he said it to the newspapers. He even said it on television.

"I don't know what's happening," he said. "But I wish I did. If it goes on, we'll be thrown out of the league. And we can't have that."

"No, we can't," said Aidan's mum, who was watching television with Aidan. "I've got two tickets for Saturday's match, if you want them. It's hard to get them these days. Everyone wants to come, just to see what the ball does next."

Chapter 2
The New Boy

At Aidan's school the next day,
everyone was talking about Lowgate.

Tall Terry, who was brainy, said that
the police had searched the Directors'
Box looking for a remote control device.
Bossy Billie said Lowgate would be
kicked out of the league.

Then, nosy Nina said, "Who's that?"
and everyone looked at a new boy in
the corner.

He was skinny, with shiny black hair, blue eyes, and a very new school uniform. Aidan went to talk to him because nobody else did.

"I'm Liam," said the new boy. He had a friendly grin. "We've just moved from the other side of town. What's it like here?"

They talked about teachers, and school dinners, and sport, and brothers and sisters, and Lowgate, because Liam supported them, too.

Soon they were such good friends that Aidan knew what he wanted to do with his match tickets.

"I've got tickets for Saturday," he said. "Lowgate against Millworth. Want to come?"

"Cool!" said Liam.

On a Saturday so cold that icicles hung from the Jam Street gates, Aidan and Liam stood in the queue. They stamped their feet on the frosty ground. Liam's ears were bright pink with cold.

"Look out," Aidan said to Liam. "There's Wendy."

"Who?" asked Liam.

"Washing Wendy," whispered Aidan. "She's Mum's friend. She's in charge of the laundry here."

"What!" said Liam. "You mean she washes the kit for Keith Connolly, and Hackett, and — "

"Yes," said Aidan, "She's nice, but she fusses a lot. And she's seen us. Here she comes!"

Wendy wore a huge anorak and a Lowgate scarf. She had a very loud voice.

"Hello, Aidan!" she boomed. "Who's your friend?"

"This is Liam, from my class," said Aidan, turning red.

"We're going to win, aren't we, Liam?" said Wendy. "What do you think? Two-nil? Three-nil? Liam, son, you look frozen. Haven't you got a hat? There's an old one in the laundry."

She elbowed her way through the crowd and soon came back with a woolly Lowgate hat.

It had lost its shape, and was too big for Liam.

"It's been lying around for ages," she called out, as if she wanted the world to hear. "Don't worry, son, I washed it."

She pulled it over Liam's ears, and he pushed it up so he could see.

At last the queue began to move, and Liam and Aidan found their seats. The players ran on, the whistle blew, and the match started.

Reporters scribbled notes and talked into mobile phones. They were watching for anything suspicious.

Near the end of the first half, Millworth found a gap in the Lowgate defence. Suddenly, it looked dangerous. Aidan yelled and cheered for Lowgate. Liam shouted something in his ear. Something about a dog.

Aidan tried to hear.

"Why don't they get that dog off the pitch?" yelled Liam.

"What dog?" Aidan shouted back. There was a surge of noise as the ball curled towards the Lowgate goal. The keeper leapt the wrong way. The ball shot for the open goal ...

... and stopped. It simply stopped in mid-air and landed on the pitch.

The Lowgate defence cleared it.

The Millworth crowd booed.

"Did you see that?" said Liam.

"Everybody saw that," said Aidan.

"I don't get it," said Liam. "Why didn't the ref get that dog off the pitch?"

Aidan wondered if there was
something strange about Liam.
"There isn't any dog," he said.
He looked again, to make sure.
"There's no dog!"

Chapter 3

"Don't You Believe Me?"

At half time, Liam told Aidan what he'd seen. "A dog ran on when Lowgate were in trouble," he said. "It stopped the ball when it was heading for the goal. Didn't you see it?"

Aidan wondered if Liam was joking, but his friend looked truly puzzled. "*You've* seen this dog. But nobody else has," Aidan said.

Aidan lowered his voice. "Do you mean that all the odd things are caused by an invisible dog?"

"Yes," said Liam. "Don't you believe me?"

"I suppose so," said Aidan. "But what shall we do? We ought to tell somebody."

"But they'll think we're crazy if we talk about invisible dogs playing football," said Liam.

Aidan could see he had a point. "Do you think it's a ghost?" he said.

"It doesn't *look* like a ghost," said Liam. "It just looks like a small terrier. Nice dog."

"Well, it's a nice dog that's going to get us booted out of the league," muttered Aidan.

In the second half, play was fast and tough. Lowgate scored. The pace grew faster.

Millworth surged forward.

"There's the dog!" yelled Liam.

Millworth had the ball. With a sharp, accurate strike, the ball shot through a defender's legs towards the Lowgate goal.

"He's after it – he's got it!" said Liam.

The ball stopped long enough for the keeper to race out and clear it.

"That ball should have gone in," said Aidan.

The game ended with a Lowgate win. But even the Lowgate players didn't look pleased. The Millworth fans went away with grim faces.

"We'll wait for Mum," said Aidan, glumly.

They trudged upstairs to the staff room, where the walls were covered in faded pictures. There were footballers in baggy shorts, and a few sad old men who might have been directors.

The television in the corner was already showing match reports and interviews.

"Lowgate never loses at home," said the reporter. "Are they cheating, or aren't they? Today, their luck was astonishing."

"We all want Lowgate to win, but it has to be fair," said Liam. "That dog thinks it's helping by playing for us."

"Could we train it not to?" said
Aidan.

"Train a ghost dog?" said Liam. "I
don't know. I've only trained a live
one."

Then Wendy marched in with three
mugs of hot chocolate on a tray and
Aidan decided she wasn't so bad.

"It's cold enough to freeze your
boots to your feet," she said. "It'll be
frozen hard for the friendly game on
Wednesday. Of course, these days, they
have heating under the pitch. It was
never like that in the old days."

She looked up at one of the photographs. "I don't know what Jack McGregor would think about it."

"Who?" asked Aidan.

Wendy cupped her hands around a mug and nodded at the picture.

It showed a man with stooped shoulders and a lined face. He looked as if he might smile at any moment.

"That's Jack," she said. "He was the groundsman here for years. He went on working till they had to carry him off the pitch, bless him. He kept it lovely. On a winter morning, you'd see Jack out there, sweeping snow, with the fans helping. His little dog used to run on ahead to catch snowballs."

"Ouch!" said Aidan, as hot chocolate splashed on to his leg. "Sorry, you made me jump. Did you say 'dog'?"

Wendy shrugged. "Yes, his name was Bobby. He was some sort of terrier," she said. "It was a while ago, so I can't properly remember."

She finished her drink. "The players will have changed by now," she said. "There'll be a mountain of dirty kits for me to wash."

"That's it!" said Liam, when she had gone. "I bet it was Jack McGregor's dog that I saw!"

"So why didn't I see him?" said Aidan. "And how can we keep him off the pitch?"

Chapter 4
The Plan

Wednesday evening at Jam Street was bitterly cold, even for Liam and Aidan with their Lowgate scarves, hats, and jackets.

This time, they had a plan. In Liam's pocket was a bag of doggie chocolate drops. Maybe, Bobby would find those more interesting than the football.

They could feed them to him slowly, one by one, all through the match.

In case that didn't work – or if they ran out of chocolate drops – Aidan had a ball in his pocket.

Their seats were near the front, so they could attract Bobby's attention.

A large man was sitting in front of Aidan, so Aidan sat on the steps at the end of the row.

The man glared at him. He had a red face and very small eyes.

"Sitting on the steps is not allowed," he ordered.

He looked like someone you shouldn't argue with, so Aidan moved back to his seat.

"Where's the dog?" he whispered to Liam.

"Beside the players' tunnel," Liam whispered back. "How can we get near him? Look out, someone's coming."

A smartly-dressed man came briskly towards them. "He's a director," whispered Aidan, who'd seen him before. The director shook hands with the red-faced man.

"Very kind of you to come, Mr Pimm," he said. "We're delighted to have a visitor from the Ministry of Sport."

"Never mind that," grunted the red-faced man. "If Lowgate are cheating, I'll find out."

Liam turned sharply to Aidan.
"Bobby's heading for the main
entrance!" he whispered. "Quick, Aidan!"

Chapter 5

"What Are You Two Doing?"

Aidan and Liam dashed for the entrance. Liam dodged behind a drinks stall and Aidan followed.

"He's here!" said Liam. He pushed up the woolly hat that was almost over his eyes and took the chocolate drops from his pocket.

"Bobby!" he whispered. "Bobby! Choccy!" It didn't seem to be working.

Liam stuffed the chocolate back in his pocket.

"He was sniffing at something, but it wasn't the chocolate," he told Aidan. "I suppose ghosts don't eat it."

"Maybe you just smell funny," said Aidan. "I mean, to a dog. Where is he now?"

"Still there," said Liam, and pushed his hat up again. "I can't see a thing with this hat on."

"Try mine," said Aidan, and they swapped hats.

Aidan was folding back the woolly hat when Liam said, "He's vanished!"

In the empty space in front of him, Aidan suddenly saw a small dog. Its tail was wagging and its head was on one side.

"Bobby?" said Aidan. "Liam, I can see him!" Aidan looked at Liam.

"It's the hat!" said Aidan.

"If you wear that hat, you see Bobby!" said Liam. Bobby pawed Aidan's leg and looked hopefully up at the hat.

"He likes that hat," said Liam.
"Can we take him somewhere quiet?
He might play with the hat and forget
the match."

"For ninety minutes and extra time?"
said Aidan. "We can try. There's a yard
behind the laundry where Wendy
hangs the washing."

Bobby trotted after them with bright
eyes fixed on the hat.

"Come on, Bobby," said Aidan, and took off the hat.

The dog disappeared at once, but he felt something tugging the hat.

"He's playing tug of war," Aidan called, as the hat thrashed in his hands. "If he'd let go, I'd throw it for him."

"Bobby!" ordered Liam. "Give!"

Bobby let go and suddenly Liam grabbed the hat. He threw it. "Fetch!" he called. The hat turned in the air and dropped at his feet.

It was working. Bobby had a great time playing fetch and tug of war. Chanting and cheering came from the ground.

The cheering grew louder. From the pitch came a roar that could only mean one thing.

"Lowgate scored!" said Aidan.

But Bobby had heard the cheers, too.
The hat turned and flew towards the
stand, with Liam and Aidan racing
after it.

"Bobby!" yelled Liam, as the hat
headed for the pitch. Soon, everyone
would see it. Aidan ran so fast that
his lungs hurt.

Then an enormous shape blocked the boys' way.

It was Mr Pimm. Aidan and Liam stopped, out of breath.

"What have you two been doing?" he growled.

"We're chasing my friend's hat," panted Aidan.

"Oh? Grown legs and run away, has it?" sneered Mr Pimm.

Aidan wanted to say that it had blown away, but there was no wind.

"A dog ran off with it," he said.

"I didn't see a dog," he said. "They're not allowed in here." He turned to Liam, who was trying to see round him. "What are you looking at?"

"My hat," said Liam. "It's lying beside the stand. The dog must have dropped it."

"Stay there!" ordered Mr Pimm.

Mr Pimm went to snatch up the hat, and came back examining it.

"May I have it back, please?" said Liam, politely.

"*I'm* holding on to this hat," said Mr Pimm. "There's something funny going on. You two can sit with me, where I can keep an eye on you."

They trudged back to their seats.

Aidan knew that without Liam's hat to play with, Bobby would join in the match.

Soon, a shot heading for the Lowgate goal stopped in mid air.

Then it rolled to a defender's feet.

All through the second half, the ball seemed to be playing for Lowgate. Lowgate won, but nobody felt very good about it.

"Can I have my hat, please?" asked Liam. Mr Pimm handed it back crossly.

"I don't know what you two are up to," said Mr Pimm. "But nothing strange happened until you arrived."

"That doesn't prove anything," said Aidan.

"Don't be cheeky," said Mr Pimm. "When you came back to your seats, things began to go wrong. You two are coming to the match against Pitch Park on Saturday."

"Wow!" said Aidan.

"Thanks!" said Liam.

"Don't look so pleased," went on Mr Pimm. "I think you're up to something. You'll be sitting next to me. I'll be watching you, in case anything strange happens."

"We're stuck," Aidan said to Liam afterwards. "If we have to sit with Mr Pimm, we can't stop Bobby."

"And Lowgate will get kicked out of the league," said Liam. "Our names will be in the clear, but Lowgate's won't."

"We'll think of something," said Aidan.

On Saturday, the game was about to begin and Liam was wearing the hat. But they still hadn't thought of anything at all.

Chapter 6

The Last Game

"Bobby's behind the goal," said Liam. "He's ready for action."

"And we can't stop him," said Aidan. "Here comes Mr Pimm."

"Swap hats?" said Liam. "I can't bear to watch."

Aidan put on the hat. He saw the bright-eyed little dog watching the pitch and he knew why Liam couldn't bear to watch. Bobby really wanted to help.

"Shall we tell Mr Pimm?" he said.
"We could let him try on the hat."

They watched Mr Pimm pushing
through the crowd, looking grumpier
than ever.

"No chance," they both said. Aidan
stared at Bobby, trying to think of some
way to keep him out of the match.

It was impossible.

"Aidan!" said Liam, sharply. He pointed to the opposite stand. "Look! It's him!"

A steward was pushing a wheelchair towards the bottom of the stand. In the chair sat an old, old man with a cap on his head, a Lowgate scarf round his neck, and a rug over his knees.

He smiled as if the smile went all the way down inside.

"It's Jack McGregor!" said Aidan. "I thought he was dead!"

"Well, he can't be, because he's here," said Liam. "Wendy said he had to be carried off the pitch, but that doesn't mean he's dead, does it? He might be living in an old people's home somewhere. He's here today as a treat."

He frowned. "Where's Bobby?"

"Halfway across the pitch!" said Aidan.

Bobby was tearing across the grass, his little tail wagging furiously.

He scrabbled to a stop at the wheelchair.

Then he put his paws on the old man's knees.

Jack McGregor simply looked down and smiled. He stretched out a frail, shaky hand and laid it on the rug.

"Bobby's licking Jack's hand, isn't he?" said Liam.

"Yes," said Aidan, excitedly. "And Jack can see him! Wendy never knew whose hat this was, did she?"

"No," said Liam, "but I bet it was Jack's. Do you think Bobby's going to behave now?"

"If anyone can control him, Jack can," said Aidan. Then the players ran down the tunnel, and the game kicked off.

It was a tough game. By half time, Pitch Park were a goal up.

Whatever Lowgate's manager, Big Brian, said to the team at half time, it worked. In the second half, they played like lightning.

Bobby lay at Jack's feet with his eyes raised to his old master's face. Now and then he sat up to lick the thin hand. Jack would look down and smile, and stroke his head.

The final whistle blew. Lowgate had won 2–1. And there was no doubt about the result. It was a fair win.

Through the cheering, Liam shouted to Aidan, "The hat!"

Aidan gave it to him. They wriggled through the crowd until they stood in front of the wheelchair.

"Excuse me, Jack – Mr McGregor," said Liam. "I think this is your hat."

Aidan bent down. "He's a nice dog," he whispered into the old man's ear.

Jack McGregor's eyes twinkled with secret laughter.

He was smiling down at something on one side of his chair, as the steward wheeled him away.

"Bobby's going home with Jack," said Aidan. "Do you think he'll come back?"

"No," said Liam. "That's what he was waiting for. He was waiting for Jack to come back for him."

"I'll miss him," said Aidan. "But it's a good thing he's gone."

There were no more strange happenings at Jam Street after that. Mr Pimm said the trouble must have been caused by the heating system under the pitch.

It wasn't Lowgate's fault, he said, but they were not allowed to use it any more.

The Lowgate directors were a bit cross. They'd spent a lot of money on the heating system. Apart from that, everyone was very glad. Nobody suspected Lowgate of cheating now.

"What will they do without the heating," said Liam, "next time it snows before a match?"

"What they used to do," said Aidan. "Get the fans to help clear the pitch."

"We could do that," said Liam.

"Yeah," said Aidan. "Jack would be pleased!"

About the author

I'm not sure where this story came from but I very much wanted to do a book about football. I imagined a game where the ball appears to move by magic.

I never used to know much about football, but it's amazing how much my sons have taught me.

I like Bobby a lot – and Wendy. Have you ever wondered who washes all that muddy kit?